What the Arabic words mean:
rababa – a one-stringed Bedouin instrument which accompanies sung poetry.
Ahlan wa sahlan! – Welcome!

Azad's Camel copyright © Frances Lincoln Limited 2009
Text and illustrations copyright © Erika Pal 2009

First published in Great Britain in 2009 and the USA in 2010 by
Frances Lincoln Children's Books, 4 Torriano Mews,
Torriano Avenue, London NW5 2RZ
www.franceslincoln.com

British Library Cataloguing in Publication Data available on request

ISBN: 978-1-84507-982-6

Illustrated with watercolour and inks

Set in HelveticaNeue

Printed in China

1 3 5 7 9 8 6 4 2

Azad's Camel

Erika Pal

F

FRANCES LINCOLN
CHILDREN'S BOOKS

Somewhere in Arabia, in a village near a big city,
lived a little orphan boy called Azad.

Azad lived with his old uncle. He fetched water to make their tea and looked after their goat.

In the afternoon, Azad would meet his friends to play.
Azad did handstands on the goalpost – he was brilliant!

One day a rich sheikh drove by.
He was amazed by Azad's balancing skill.

Later the sheikh visited Azad's uncle.
"Let me take the boy," he said. "I will train him
to become a camel rider. One day he'll be famous."

"Take him, and good luck to you,"
said Azad's uncle. "I can't afford to keep him."
So the next morning, Azad drove away with the sheikh.

The sheikh took Azad to a tent where lots of other children were sleeping. Before he left, he hissed into Azad's ear, "You'll hear strange stories about talking camels and wandering people of the desert. Take my advice: don't listen to them!

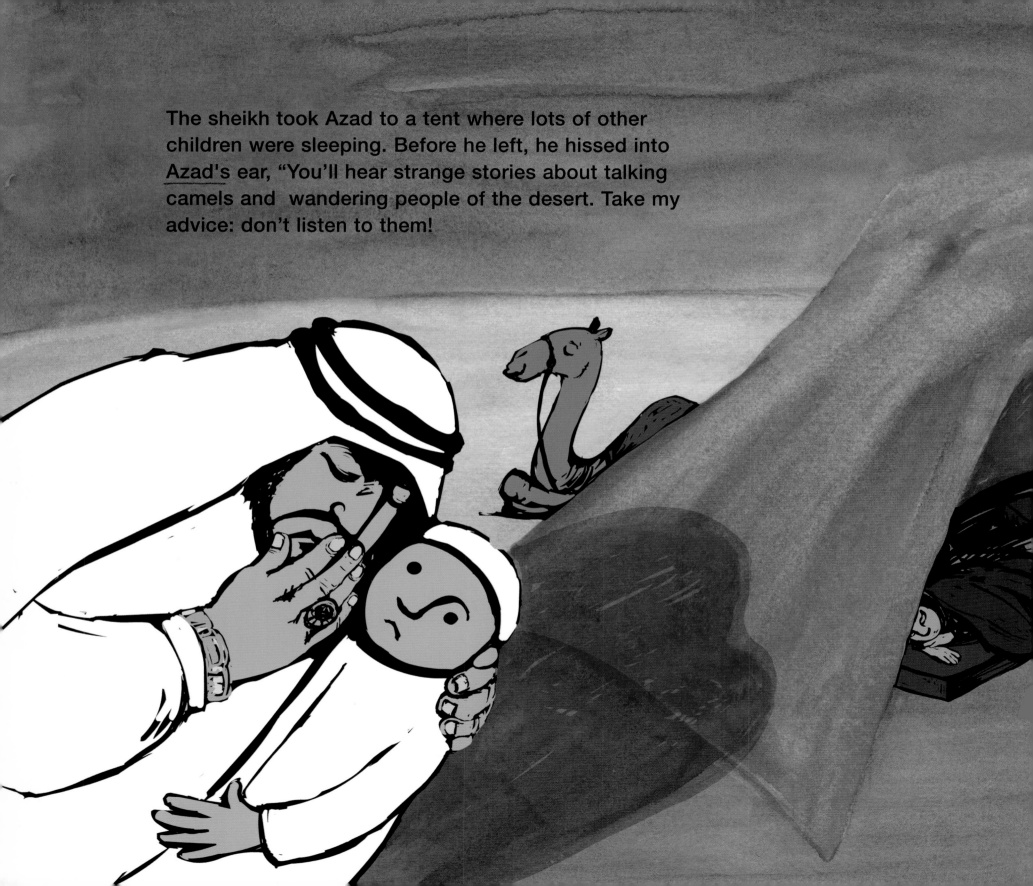

Early the next morning, a man came in and shouted at the children: "Wake up, you lazybones! Go and feed the camels!"

"May I have some breakfast, please?"
Azad asked shyly.
The man burst out laughing.
"Here, you have to earn your breakfast!"
he yelled.

"It's time for your first riding lesson. Let's see
how long you can stay on a camel's back!"
"I can't ride!" cried Azad, but it was too late.

The camel started to run very fast.
Azad closed his eyes and hung on tightly.

But he didn't fall off...

The trainer was impressed, and entered Azad in a camel race that day. It was the first of many...

The races were dangerous.
Azad was frightened by the camels' blazing speed,
and deafened by their thundering hooves and the
shouts of the crowd.
He did not like racing at all.

Often Azad couldn't get to sleep afterwards. He would sit outside for hours watching the stars.
One night a strange voice said: "What are you doing here?"
Azad looked up. It was his camel, Asfur.
"You're talking!"
"Of course. I'm just choosy about who I talk to."

"I don't want to race tomorrow," said Azad. "I'm scared."
"Me too," sighed Asfur. "And one day I won't be as fast as
I am now, and I'll end up on the sheikh's dinner table."
"That's awful!" said Azad. "How can we escape?"
"Hmmm," replied the camel. "I think I know where to go.
Just hold on very tight tomorrow."

The next day at the races, Azad and his camel crossed
the finishing line first! But this time they did not stop.
Asfur went on running.
"Stop!" screamed the sheikh.
"Come back!" yelled the trainer...

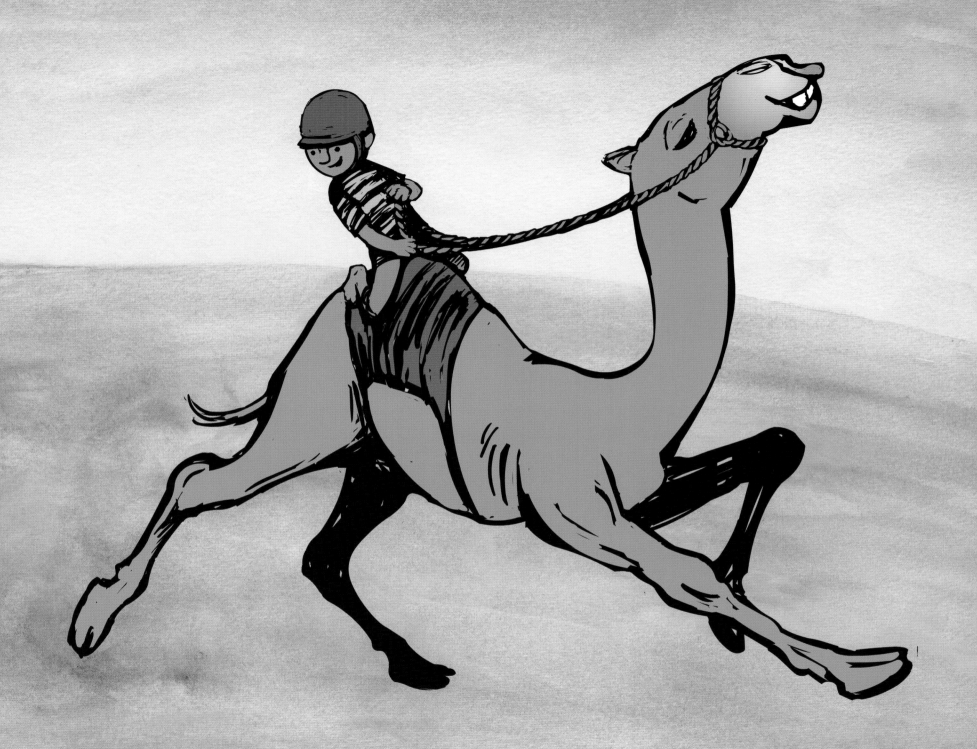

but Azad and Asfur were too fast.

They ran all the way through the city.

At last they reached the desert. It was night,
and no one was chasing them any more.

It grew colder and colder.
Worn out, Azad and Azfur fell asleep in the freezing desert.
But they were not alone…

All around them, animals appeared out of the darkness.

Oryx gazelles, desert foxes and a sand cat
huddled together to keep them warm.

At the crack of dawn they vanished behind the dunes.

When Azad opened his eyes, he saw two smiling faces
looking down at him.
"*Ahlan wa sahlan!* Welcome, travellers!" said one of them.
"You have come a long way, my friends!"

That evening, as Azad and Asfur sat with the Bedouin
around the fire, one of them played on his *rababa*.
He sang about a brave little boy and his camel...

...who had found a home at last.

About camel racing

Camel racing is a popular sport in the Gulf states of the Middle East. Child jockeys are used to ride the camels and come from Pakistan, Bangladesh, Sudan, Mauritania and Eritrea. Some poor families are persuaded to sell sons as young as five years old, who are taken away to be trained and often badly treated. Accidents happen a lot, and when a little jockey falls off a racing camel, he can receive serious injuries.

Qatar, Oman and the United Arab Emirates have banned the use of child jockeys and are returning the children to their families so that they can go to school and live a normal life. Most children look forward to going back, but some do not want to return to stepfathers or families who sold them in the first place, and other homes have to be found for them.

Robots are now being used instead of jockeys in the United Arab Emirates, but in some Middle Eastern countries small children are still being forced to race camels, and the trade in child smuggling continues.

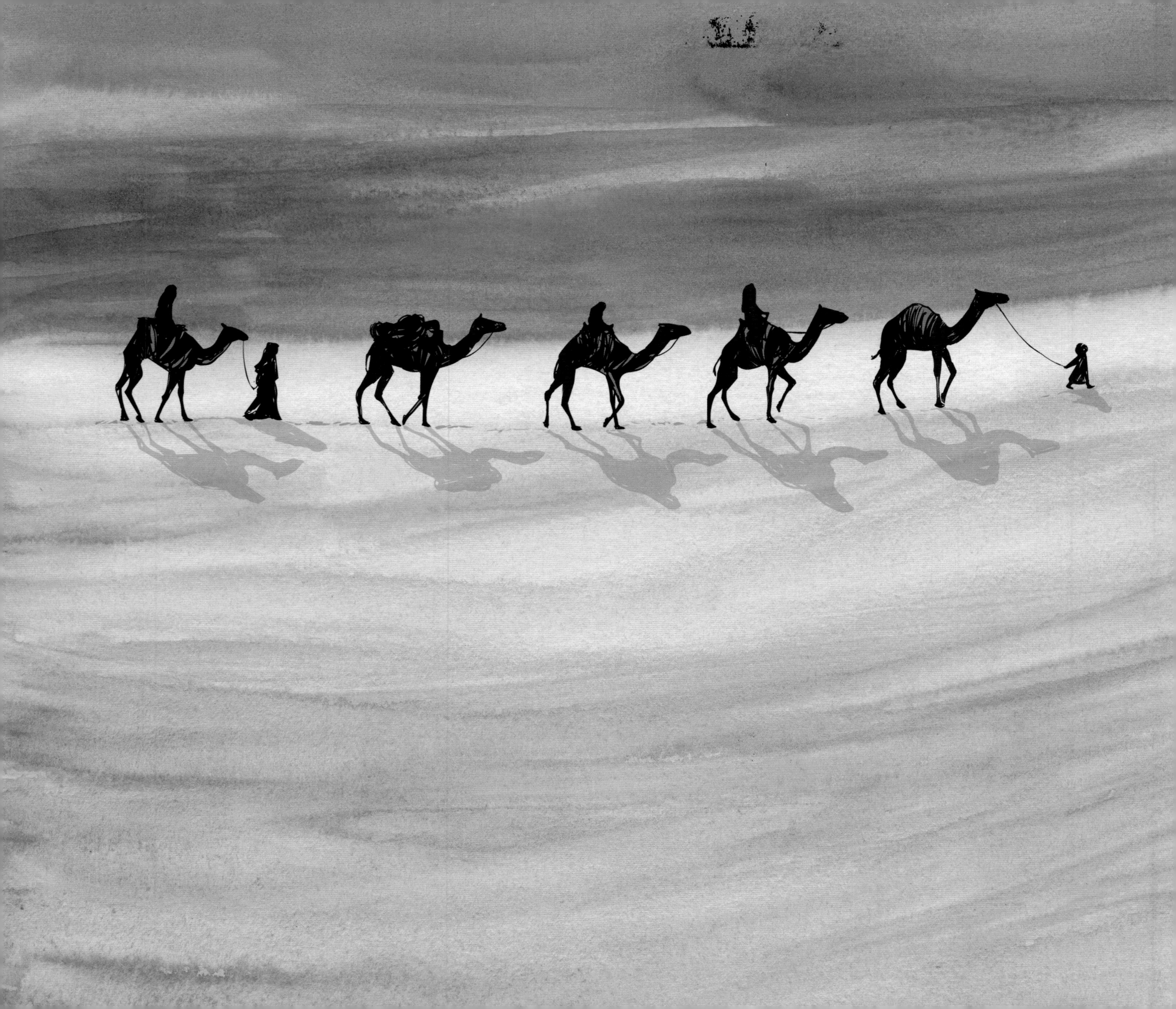